MILE END

DISCARD

To urban kids around the world who illuminate
concrete alleys with their brimming imaginations,
starting with Arnaud and Florent, my own
two Mile Enders and inspiration

Special thanks to my friend and agent, Kirsten Hall, whose sense
of wonder and intuition guided me toward this adventure

Copyright © 2017 by Isabelle Arsenault

All rights reserved. Published in the United States by Random House Children's Books,
a division of Penguin Random House LLC, New York. Published simultaneously in Canada
by Tundra Books, Toronto, in 2017.

Random House and the colophon are registered trademarks of Penguin Random House LLC.

Visit us on the Web! randomhousekids.com

Educators and librarians, for a variety of teaching tools, visit us at RHTeachersLibrarians.com

Library of Congress Cataloging-in-Publication Data is available upon request.

ISBN 978-0-553-53659-1 (trade) — ISBN 978-0-553-53660-7 (lib. bdg.) —
ISBN 978-0-553-53661-4 (ebook)

MANUFACTURED IN CHINA

10 9 8 7 6 5 4 3 2 1

First American Edition

Edited by Tara Walker and Maria Modugno
Designed by Isabelle Arsenault and Kelly Hill
The artwork in this book was rendered in pencils, watercolor, and ink
with digital coloration in Photoshop.
Hand-lettering by Isabelle Arsenault

A Mile End Kids Story

COLETTE'S LOST PET

Words and pictures by
ISABELLE ARSENAULT

Random House New York

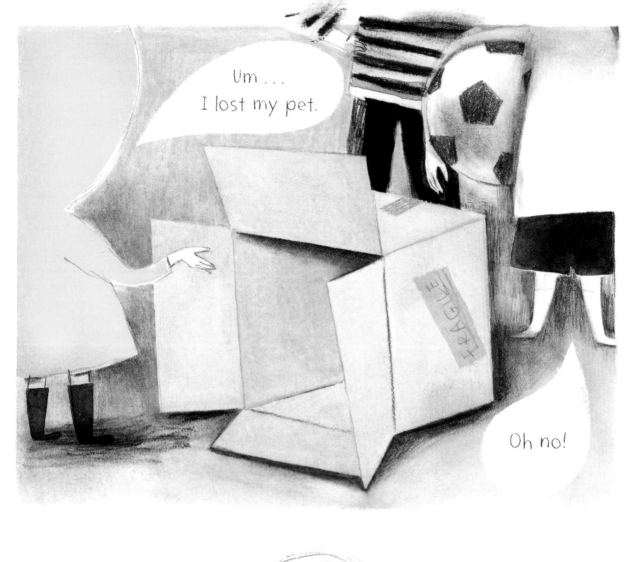

Um . . .
I lost my pet.

Oh no!

Is it
a dog?

Or a cat?

Hey, Lily!

Have you seen
Colette's lost pet?
It's a parakeet.

Gee, that's not
the kind of bird
I usually see around
here. What color is it?

Um, well . . .

uhhh . . . It's blue!

With a bit
of yellow on
its neck.

Hey, Scott!

Have you seen Colette's lost pet?
It's a parakeet. It's blue with a
bit of yellow on its neck.

Oh, what's
its name?

Um,
well . . .

uh . . . Marie.

Marie-Antoinette!
Like the princess.

Hey, Maya!

Prrrr
uiiiii

Have you seen Colette's lost pet?
It's a parakeet. It's blue with a
bit of yellow on its neck, and its
name is Marie-Antoinette.

What does it
sound like?

Um, well . . . uh . . .

Like PRrrrrrr
Prrrr PrrrrrruiiiiiiT!

And it speaks a
little bit, too.

But only
in French.

Bien sûr!

Aw, cute! I haven't heard it but I did hear Beth's cat meowing. It passed by just a minute ago . . . .

Oh!

To Beth's!

Don't worry, Colette. We'll find Marie-Annette!

Marie-Antoinette!

Hey, Beth!

Have you seen Colette's lost pet?
It's a parakeet. It's blue with a bit
of yellow on its neck, its name is
Marie-Antoinette and it makes
a sound like PRrrrrr
Prrrr PrrrrrruiiiiiiT!

I don't think so.
Do you have a picture
of it?

Um, well . . .

uh . . .

Too bad I don't
have that great shot
we took in . . .

uh, Hawaii.

I can draw it
though!

Hey, Lukas!

Have you seen Colette's lost pet? It's a parakeet. It's blue with
a bit of yellow on its neck, its name is Marie-Antoinette,
it makes a sound like PRrrrrrr Prrrr PrrrrrruiiiiiiT
and it SURFS! See this drawing? Can you
help us make it into a poster?

Let me see.
Is this your bird's
actual size?

Um, well ... uh ...

yes, pretty much,
I guess.

But ...

It's gained
some weight
lately . . . .

It kind of
grew bigger

and bigger.

So I had to get
a bigger cage

and then a
bigger house.

Until it became <u>TOO BIG</u> to fit in the house!

But then it was the perfect size to fly around!

So we traveled the world.

I'm telling you,
this parakeet is <u>truly</u>
amazing!

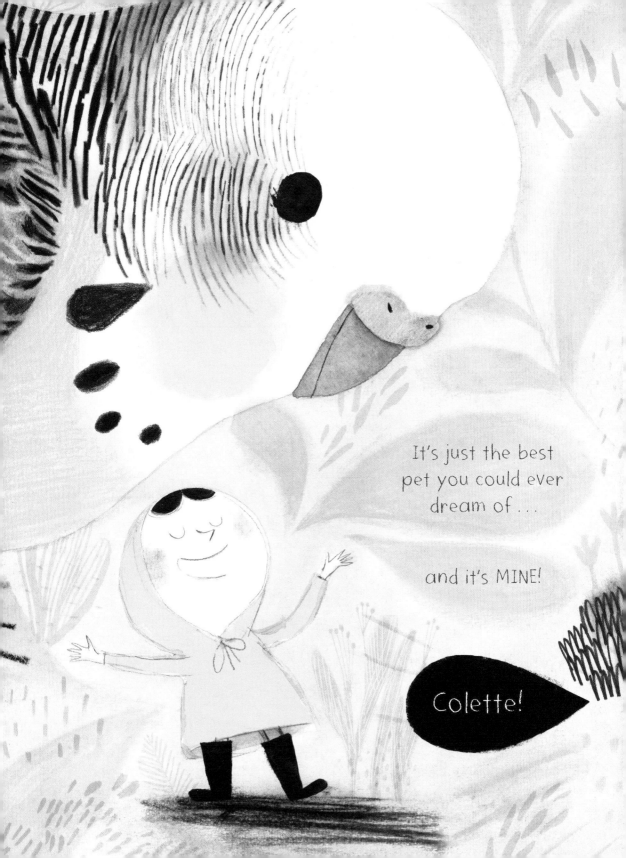

It's just the best
pet you could ever
dream of . . .

and it's MINE!

Colette!

Um . . . well, okay!

I'll tell you more later!

Can't wait!

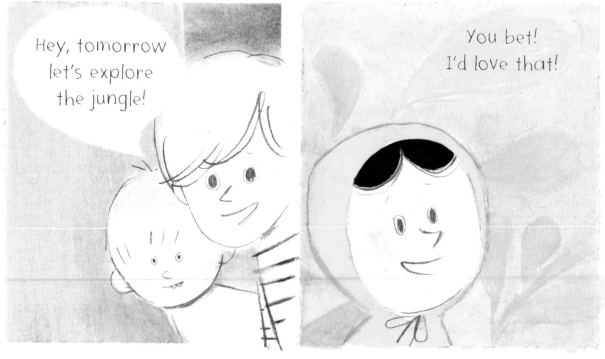

Hey, tomorrow let's explore the jungle!

You bet! I'd love that!

CLARK ALLEY